Here's what kids, parents, and teachers have to say to Ron Roy, author of the A to Z Mysteries series:

"I really enjoy reading your books. They are filled with fun, excitement, and joy."—Olivia S.

"I wish I could spend time with Dink, Josh, and Ruth Rose to help them solve crimes." —Jonathan G.

"I love your A to Z Mystery books. They are exciting, and they have good solutions, because they never turn out the way you think they will."—Bridget L.

"Keep on writing! I'd be *soooooooooooo* sad if you quit!"—Lesley S.

"[My son] loves that Josh is so funny, Dink is so understanding, and Ruth Rose is so smart. Thank you for writing these wonderful books that have so captured Richard's interest." —Claire V.

"My class and I love your books! It is refreshing to have a series of books that contain many teachable elements." —Angela E.

*This book is for all my readers who have sent me
letters and e-mails. Thank you!*
—R.R.

To the immortal Bela Lugosi
—J.S.G.

ISBN 0-439-68090-5

Text copyright © 2004 by Ron Roy. Illustrations copyright © 2004 by John Steven Gurney.
All rights reserved. Published by Scholastic Inc., 557 Broadway, New York, NY 10012,
by arrangement with Random House Children's Books, a division of Random House, Inc.
SCHOLASTIC and associated logos are trademarks and/or registered trademarks of Scholastic Inc.

24 23 22 21 20 19 18 17 16 15 14 13   8 9/0

Printed in the U.S.A.   40

First Scholastic printing, November 2004

A to Z Mysteries

The Vampire's Vacation

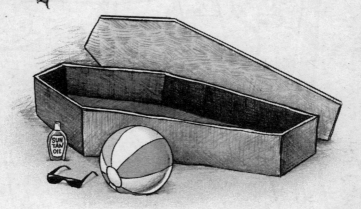

by Ron Roy

illustrated by
John Steven Gurney

SCHOLASTIC INC.

New York Toronto London Auckland Sydney
Mexico City New Delhi Hong Kong Buenos Aires

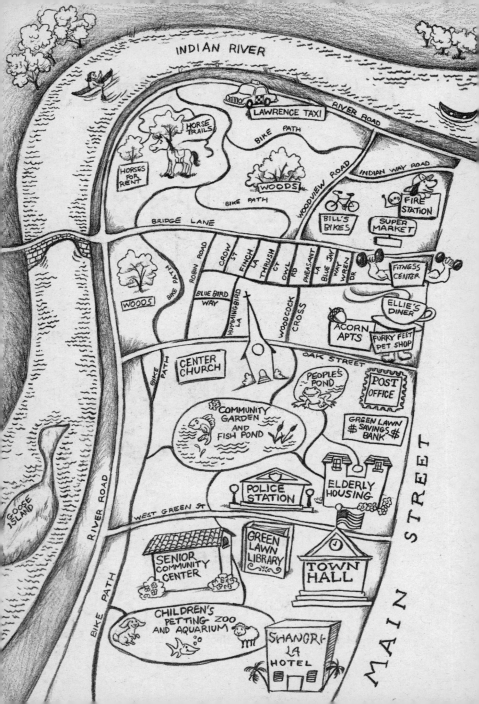

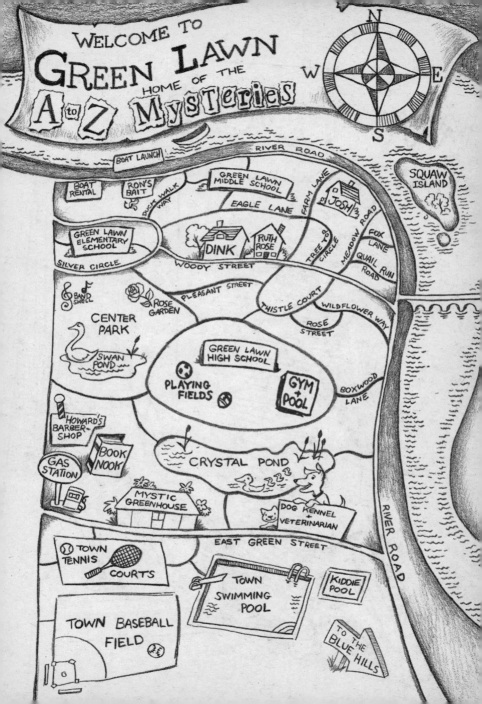

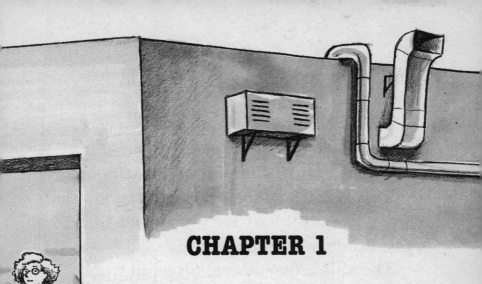

CHAPTER 1

"Careful going over the curb, or you'll spill the whole pile," Dink cautioned his friend Josh.

"You and Ruth Rose are supposed to be holding on to it!" Josh answered.

"We *are* holding, Josh," Ruth Rose said. "But you're pulling the wagon too fast!"

An hour before, Dink and Josh had helped Ruth Rose clean some old newspapers out of her basement. Now they were hauling the papers to the recycling bin at the supermarket. For the job, Ruth

Rose borrowed her little brother Nate's wagon.

It was early August and the sky was filled with cotton candy clouds. The kids wore shorts and T-shirts. Ruth Rose liked to dress all in one color. Her shorts and shirt were sky blue. They matched her eyes, headband, and sneakers.

The kids crossed Main Street in front of the supermarket. "Almost there," Dink said, struggling to keep the tower of papers from toppling. A drop of sweat fell from the tip of his nose.

Dink's real name was Donald David Duncan. Most people called him Dink, except his mother when she was annoyed with him.

The kids tugged the wagon to a row of tall wooden bins at the side of the supermarket. Each bin was labeled according to what was being recycled, and one was for newspapers.

Dink pulled open the door, and the

kids began tossing bundles of papers inside.

"Boy, was that hard work," Josh announced when they were finished. He grabbed the wagon handle. "Let's go inside and get something to drink!"

Dink and Ruth Rose followed Josh into the supermarket. The automatic door swooshed open, and they were immediately bathed in cool air.

They found a machine in the frozen-foods section and each bought a cold soda.

"Guys, look!" Josh whispered. He tipped his soda can toward the meat counter. A few customers waited while a butcher sliced steaks.

"Why are we looking at steaks?" Dink asked.

"You're always thinking of your next meal, Josh," said Ruth Rose.

"No, I mean the guy standing there," Josh said. He pointed at a man dressed

completely in black. His slicked-back hair was also black. His skin was ghostly pale. Dark sunglasses were perched above his long nose.

"I wonder who he is," Josh said. "I've never seen him in Green Lawn before."

"I haven't, either," Dink said. "But so

what? I don't know everybody in town."

Ruth Rose peeked over a display of frozen chickens to get a better look. "Something about him looks familiar," she said.

"Do you know what he looks like to me?" Josh asked.

"A man buying meat?" Dink said.

Josh shook his head. "No. He looks like a vampire!"

Dink grinned at Josh. "Have you ever *seen* a vampire, Josh?" he asked.

"No, but I know what they look like." Josh pointed toward the man. "Vampires have skinny lips and really pale skin, like him!"

Ruth Rose laughed. "Your skin is pale. Are you a vampire?" she asked.

"I am not pale," Josh said. "I have freckles."

The man strolled away from the meat counter.

"Let's follow him!" Josh said.

"Why?" Dink asked.

"Because he's weird!" Josh said. "Who wears sunglasses inside a store?"

"Lots of people do, Josh," Dink said.

"Guys, we have to go home for more newspapers," Ruth Rose said. "My mom is paying us, remember?"

"We can do that later," Josh said, finishing his drink. "Come on, the guy's leaving!"

Shaking their heads, Dink and Ruth Rose followed Josh, who took off after the man in black.

Suddenly the man stopped in the doorway. He turned and seemed to stare right at the three kids. The store lights reflected off his glasses like tiny lightning bolts. The man smiled and nodded at the kids.

Dink, Josh, and Ruth Rose froze. The man in black shoved the door open and walked out.

"Oh my gosh," Josh whispered. "He saw us following him!"

"No, he saw *you* following him," Ruth Rose said. "I'm going home to help my mom."

"The guy *is* pretty strange," Dink said. "I got goose bumps when he looked at us."

"That's because it's air-conditioned in here," Ruth Rose said. "Can we go now?"

"I want to see where he's going," Josh said. Crouching, he pulled the wagon through the door. Dink and Ruth Rose were right behind him, laughing.

The stranger made his way down Main Street. The kids stayed behind him. Suddenly he disappeared inside a doorway.

"He's gone into Ellie's!" Josh said.

"Gee, I didn't know vampires ate real food," Dink cracked. "Don't they just drink blood?"

Josh ignored Dink. "We're going in, too," Josh said. "But let's wait a couple of minutes. We don't want to look like we're following him."

"But we are!" Ruth Rose pointed out.

"Well, we don't have to advertise it!" Josh said. "Let's just get ice cream, like we usually do."

The kids left the wagon outside and pushed through the door to Ellie's Diner. Ellie had her back to them. The kids glanced around at all the seats. The man in black was nowhere to be seen.

"Where'd he go?" Josh whispered.

"Are you sure he came in here?" Dink asked. "Maybe he went into the pet shop next door."

"I know he came in here," Josh said.

He peeked under a booth. "Let's ask Ellie."

"Ask me what?" Ellie asked.

She turned around just as she finished sticking a small, round Band-Aid on the side of her neck.

CHAPTER 2

"Did a guy all dressed in black come in?" Josh asked.

Ellie looked confused. "In my diner? When?"

"Just a minute ago. He had black hair and pale skin," Dink said.

Ellie shook her head. "I don't know," she said. "He might have. I was out back getting supplies."

"I saw him walk in here," Josh said, peering over the counter.

"Well, he's not here now," Dink said. "Let's get some ice cream."

Ellie followed them to a booth. "Cones all around?" she asked the kids. "Your usual flavors?"

The kids all nodded, and a few minutes later, Ellie brought three cones. Butter crunch for Dink, pistachio for Josh, and strawberry for Ruth Rose. As they licked their cones, Josh stared through the window.

"What're you looking for?" Dink asked.

"The vampire guy," Josh said.

"He's not a vampire, Josh," Ruth Rose said. "Everyone knows vampires sleep during the day and come out at night. They hate the sun."

"Maybe this one's on vacation," Josh said.

Dink started to laugh and nearly choked. "Josh, why would a vampire pick Green Lawn for his vacation?" he asked.

But Josh wasn't listening. He had his

nose against the window. "There he is again!" Josh shrieked.

Dink and Ruth Rose craned their necks to look. Ellie walked over to see what the commotion was about.

The man in black was crossing Main Street near the swan pond.

"Doesn't he look like a vampire to you?" Josh asked Ellie.

Ellie didn't answer. When Dink glanced at her, Ellie seemed afraid. She backed away from the window and walked behind her counter.

Josh crunched the last of his cone, then pushed his way out of the booth. "He's heading down Main Street. I'm following him," he announced. "You guys coming?"

"Sure, why not?" Ruth Rose said. "I want to be there when the vacationing vampire grabs you!"

"Can I at least finish my cone?" Dink asked. He and Ruth Rose followed Josh out to the street.

"He's going into the Book Nook," Dink told Josh.

"I wonder what vampires read when they're on vacation," Ruth Rose said,

taking the last bite of her cone.

"Let's find out," Josh said, heading for the bookstore. They stopped in front of Howard's Barbershop while Dink finished his ice cream.

Josh kept an eye on the Book Nook door. "Okay, let's go," he said as Dink wiped his mouth on his sleeve.

Dink and Ruth Rose followed him into the Book Nook.

A bell tinkled, and Mr. Paskey looked up from behind his counter. He smiled and waved at the kids.

Two teenagers were reading magazines. The only other person in the store was Mr. Paskey.

"He's not here," Dink whispered.

"I don't believe this!" Josh choked out. "The guy keeps disappearing! What does he do, walk through walls?"

"Hi, kids. Can I help you?" Mr. Paskey asked.

"Hi, Mr. Paskey," Dink said. "Did a

man wearing black just come in here?"

Mr. Paskey rubbed his neck. "No, I don't think so. But I was in the store-room for a minute or two. I suppose he could have come in, then left again."

Josh shook his head. "I was watching. He came in, but he didn't come out," he said.

"Sorry," Mr. Paskey said. He raised his eyebrows and shrugged.

"Did you kids leave this?" asked Mr. Paskey, reaching toward the cash register. He held up a twenty-dollar bill.

The kids shook their heads.

"How odd," Mr. Paskey said. "Someone left this bill on the counter." He looked at the money for a second, then shrugged again.

"Do you have any books about vampires?" Josh asked.

"I think there's one over in non-fiction," Mr. Paskey answered. "It's called *Vampires Among Us,* by Dan Starch."

The kids found the nonfiction books, then looked for *Starch*.

They found a book by Wanda Star, then one written by Peter Starkey. The space between them was empty.

"Mr. Paskey?" said Josh. "We found where the book should be, but it's gone."

Mr. Paskey walked over to the shelf. He put his finger in the space between the two books. "Now, that is peculiar," he muttered, crouching lower. "It was here an hour ago when I dusted this shelf."

When Mr. Paskey leaned over, his neck was level with Dink's eyes. As usual, Mr. Paskey wore a crisp white shirt, a necktie, and a suit jacket.

Dink smiled. *Even in this hot weather, Mr. Paskey dresses up,* he thought.

And then Dink noticed a small, round Band-Aid right above Mr. Paskey's shirt collar.

CHAPTER 3

The kids thanked Mr. Paskey and left his shop.

"I wonder who left that twenty-dollar bill on Mr. Paskey's counter," Ruth Rose said.

"I bet it was that guy! I know he went in there!" Josh griped. "People don't just vanish."

"But maybe vampires vanish," Ruth Rose said, grinning at Josh.

Dink laughed. He pretended to read a newspaper headline: "VACATIONING VAMPIRE VANISHES."

"Laugh, you guys," Josh said. "But I think that guy is definitely weird. And did you notice how Mr. Paskey didn't even think it was strange that some guy disappeared inside his shop?"

Dink thought for a minute. "Mr. Paskey's not the only one who's not acting like himself. When we saw that guy through the window in Ellie's Diner, Ellie looked afraid of something," he said.

"She was probably afraid Josh would choke because he was gobbling his ice cream so fast," Ruth Rose said. "Now can we go home? We can have lunch at my house."

A few minutes later, they reached Ruth Rose's house. They walked to the backyard with the wagon.

Ruth Rose's brother, Nate, was sitting at the picnic table. In front of him were a box of plastic action figures, some crayons, and drawing paper.

"Hey, Nate, what're you doing?" Dink asked.

"Drawing my guys," Nate said, holding up a picture. It showed Spider-Man and Superman fighting a purple monster.

"Where's Mommy?" Ruth Rose asked her brother.

"Here I am!" her mother said, popping up from the open cellar hatchway. "Thanks for taking those newspapers away," she said. "There are plenty more down here when you feel like working. I left sandwiches and lemonade in the fridge for you."

"Thanks, Mom," Ruth Rose said. "We'll take more papers later."

The kids brought their lunch to the picnic table, and Ruth Rose cleared a space. As they ate, they watched Nate trying to write words on his picture.

"Can I help?" Ruth Rose asked her brother.

"Write *'I give up,' said the monster*,"

Nate told Ruth Rose. He handed her a purple crayon.

"That's a neat color," Dink said.

"It's Party Purple," Nate told him. "And guess what? It smells like jelly-beans!"

Ruth Rose printed the words, then pointed to each one in turn as she read them aloud for her brother.

"Thanks, Ruth Rose!" said Nate. He grabbed the picture and ran to show his mother.

"I wonder if that guy we saw sleeps hanging upside down," Josh said.

"I hate to spoil your fun," Dink said. "Bats sleep that way, not people."

"And vampires aren't real," Ruth Rose said.

"Dracula was a real person," Josh said. "I read about him."

"But Dracula wasn't really a vam-pire," said Ruth Rose. "And he died a long time ago."

Josh wiggled his eyebrows. "How do we know he's really dead?"

Ruth Rose laughed. She reached into Nate's box and pulled out a miniature plastic Count Dracula. "Here he is!" she said.

"See," Josh said. "He looks just like our guy. All dressed in black."

"Except this one has long fangs," Ruth Rose said, standing the vampire on his plastic feet. Painted-on "blood" dripped from the fangs.

"The guy we're following might have fangs," Josh said. "We didn't see his teeth."

Suddenly Dink remembered something. "Guys, did you notice that Mr. Paskey was wearing a Band-Aid on his neck?" he asked.

"I did," Ruth Rose said. "A little round one, right here." She put a finger on the side of her own neck.

"Well, Ellie had one just like it on her neck," Dink went on.

Josh stopped chewing and his eyes widened.

"Swallow, Josh," Ruth Rose said.

Josh gulped, then took a swig of lemonade. "Don't you guys get it?" he asked. "Vampires bite people on their necks to get blood! I'm not kidding around anymore. I think that guy really *is* a vampire!"

"The only vampires are on TV, Joshua," Ruth Rose said.

"Who says?" Josh argued. "There are a lot of things that people don't think are real, then they turn out to be."

Dink was staring at Josh. "Like what?" he said.

Josh stared back. "Like . . . like giant squids!" he said.

"But giant squids are real," Ruth Rose said. "Scientists have found their bodies washed up on the shore. No one's found any vampire bodies that I know of."

"That doesn't mean there aren't any," Josh said. "There could be a lot of vampires that people don't know about."

"And you think that guy in black is one of them, right?" Dink said.

Josh nodded. "I'm starting to."

"Well, whoever he is, I still think I've seen him somewhere," Ruth Rose said.

"I say we try to find him again," Josh said.

"Why?" asked Dink.

"For one thing, I want to know how he keeps disappearing," Josh said. He grinned at Dink. "And I know you're curious about those Band-Aids on Ellie and Mr. Paskey."

"Okay, I admit it," Dink said. "So where do we look?"

Ruth Rose collected the paper plates and cups. "I can't believe I'm going vampire hunting," she said.

"If he's staying in town," Josh said, standing up, "the first place to check is the Shangri-la Hotel."

A few minutes later, the kids were on their way to the hotel. They kept their eyes open, but the man in black was nowhere to be seen.

When they walked into the hotel's cool lobby, Mr. Linkletter was talking on the phone. He looked up and nodded as the kids approached the counter.

Soon Mr. Linkletter hung up the phone. "Hello there," he said. "What brings you to the Shangri-la?"

"We saw a stranger in town and wondered if he's staying here," Josh plunged in.

Mr. Linkletter raised one eyebrow. "And why are you so curious about this stranger?" he asked.

Ruth Rose came to Josh's rescue. "Because he looks familiar," she said. "I'm trying to figure out where I've seen him before."

Mr. Linkletter squinted his eyes and pursed his lips. He tapped a long finger against the countertop. "Describe this person, please."

"He's dressed in black," Dink said.

"Black hair all slicked back," Josh added. "And his skin is real pale."

"Ah," said Mr. Linkletter. "That

would be Dr. Cula." He looked at his register. "A. Cula, a doctor from New York City."

"Is he in his room right now?" Ruth Rose asked.

Mr. Linkletter looked down at Ruth Rose. His mustache twitched, as if he might smile. "You know I can't tell you that," he said. "Shangri-la guests pay for privacy, and I make sure they get it."

Mr. Linkletter shut the register with a soft thud. "Was there anything else?"

"No thanks," Dink said, looking up at Mr. Linkletter. Then his mouth fell open.

Three inches to the right of Mr. Linkletter's Adam's apple was a small, round Band-Aid.

CHAPTER 4

"Th-thanks a lot, Mr. Linkletter," Dink stammered.

He hurried Josh and Ruth Rose out of the hotel. "Did you see Mr. Linkletter's neck?" he whispered when they were on the sidewalk. "He had on a Band-Aid just like Ellie's and Mr. Paskey's!"

"Are you sure?" Ruth Rose asked.

Dink put a finger on his own neck. "It was right here!" he said.

"Now do you guys believe something weird is going on?" Josh croaked. "A vampire is stalking Green Lawn! He's drinking everyone's blood! We gotta call 911!"

"Josh, calm down," Ruth Rose said. "There could be a lot of reasons for those three Band-Aids."

"Name one," Josh said.

"Mr. Linkletter could have cut himself shaving," Ruth Rose suggested.

"Okay, but Ellie didn't cut herself shaving, did she?" Josh retorted.

"It's strange that all three of them needed Band-Aids on the same day," Dink put in.

"Yeah, and the people wearing them are acting strange," Josh said. "Mr. Linkletter never gives out the names of his guests, but he did today!"

Josh squinted his eyes. "I'll bet if we looked under those Band-Aids, we'd see fang marks!"

Ruth Rose grinned. "Are you going to go back inside and ask Mr. Linkletter to take off his Band-Aid?"

"No, but we have to find this guy," Josh said. "He's already turned Ellie and Mr. Paskey and Mr. Linkletter into vampires! We have to save Green Lawn!"

"Josh, calm down," Dink said. "I agree that something weird is going on around here, but I don't think that guy is a vampire. And even if he is, what could we do about it?"

"Run him out of town!" Josh said.

Ruth Rose shook her head. "Run him out of town? How?"

Just then a shadow fell over the kids. A voice asked, "What're you guys whispering about?"

The kids jumped, and Josh let out a moan. But it was only their friend Livvy Nugent. She worked as a maid in the Shangri-la.

"Hi, Livvy," Ruth Rose said. "How are Nicole and Ned?"

"Growing like weeds and eating like

lion cubs," Livvy said. "So what's up?"

"Do you know Dr. Cula?" Dink asked. "He's staying in the hotel."

Livvy nodded. "He checked in last night from New York. Wears all black, right?" she said.

"That's him," Josh said. "Have you been inside his room?"

"Sure I have," Livvy said. "When he checked in, I took him up in the elevator."

"Um, did you happen to notice anything weird?" Josh persisted.

Livvy shook her head. "Not really," she said, starting to enter the hotel.

She stopped and turned around. "There was one strange thing," Livvy said. "As soon as we got in the room, Dr. Cula lay down on the bed. He asked me to turn up the air-conditioning to extra cold. I did, and asked him if he wanted another blanket. He said no, he'd brought his own."

Livvy lowered her voice. "When I turned around, he was lying there with his eyes closed, wrapped in a black cape!"

The three kids stared at Livvy.

She shook her head. "Poor guy must have been exhausted," she said. "He fell asleep so fast I thought he was dead!"

Livvy waggled her fingers good-bye and entered the lobby.

"Vampires sleep in cold coffins," Josh moaned. "And they wear capes!"

"Magicians and Salvation Army people also wear capes, Josh," Ruth Rose said.

"Dr. Cula could be a magician," Dink said. "That might explain how he escaped from Ellie's Diner and the Book Nook without us seeing him."

"And does he also make Band-Aids appear on people's necks?" Josh asked. "I'm going home." He started walking up Main Street.

"Why?" asked Dink. "I thought you wanted to find Dr. Cula."

"I do!" Josh said over his shoulder. "But first we need protection."

Ruth Rose looked at Dink. They both caught up to Josh. "What kind of protection?" she asked.

"Garlic!" Josh said.

"Garlic?" Dink and Ruth Rose repeated, staring at Josh.

"Vampires hate garlic," Josh said. "We have to hang some around our necks."

"Around our necks?" Dink said. "Josh, garlic stinks!"

Josh rolled his eyes. "Duh! That's what keeps the vampires away!"

CHAPTER 5

A few minutes later, the kids reached Josh's house. Josh marched around the house to the backyard.

His twin brothers, Brian and Bradley, were playing with blocks on the picnic table. Under the table, Josh's dog, Pal, was sound asleep.

"Where's Mom?" Josh asked the twins.

"I'm out here!" came a voice from the vegetable garden.

Josh ran toward his mother, yelling, "I need some garlic!"

Ruth Rose shook her head. "Do you

think Josh is serious about this vampire stuff, or is he just fooling around?" she asked Dink.

Dink shrugged. "I think he really believes that guy is a vampire," he said.

"What do *you* think?" Ruth Rose asked.

"I don't believe in vampires," Dink said. "But what about those Band-Aids?"

Dink and Ruth Rose sat at the table with Brian and Bradley. The twins each had a pile of letter blocks and were trying to make words.

"What are you spelling?" Dink asked them.

"Our names, but we don't know how to spell!" Bradley said.

"I'll help you," Ruth Rose said. "Do you know what letter your names begin with?"

"*B!*" both boys yelled. They each picked out a *B* block.

"That's right," Ruth Rose said. She

selected four more blocks to spell out B-R-I-A-N.

"That spells *Brian*," she said. She chose some more blocks and spelled B-R-A-D-L-E-Y.

Josh came and sat down with them. He had an armload of green stalks with white bulbs on one end.

"Ew!" cried Brian. "Smelly!"

"Yuck!" yelled Bradley. The two boys raced away from the table holding their noses.

"So this is what garlic looks like when it's growing," Dink said, sniffing one of the stalks.

Ruth Rose held her nose. "Did you tell your mom why you want the garlic, Josh?"

Josh grinned slyly. "I didn't tell her about Vampire Man," he said. "I just said I needed garlic for an experiment."

Josh started weaving stalks together.

"I think I'll pass on the garlic," Dink said.

"Okay, but don't try to steal mine when the vampire sneaks up on you," Josh said.

"I wish I could remember where I saw him before today," Ruth Rose said. She spelled out *Dr. Cula* with blocks.

"You forgot his first initial," Dink said. He picked up an *A* block and slid it between the *R* and *C* blocks.

Suddenly Josh dropped his garlic stalks. The blocks spelled D-R-A-C-U-L-A.

Dink and Ruth Rose stared at the word. To Dink, it seemed as if everything froze. Pal stopped his snoring.

"Now do you guys believe me?" Josh whispered.

"Well, okay," Ruth Rose said after a minute. "The letters in Dr. Cula's name also spell *Dracula*. But that's just a coincidence."

Dink let out a breath he didn't know he'd been holding. "I don't know," he said quietly. "The Band-Aids on Mr. Paskey, Ellie, and Mr. Linkletter could be a coincidence. And anyone could own a black cape. But this . . ."

Dink ran a finger along the seven blocks that spelled *Dracula*. "This *can't* be a coincidence!"

Ruth Rose sighed. "Okay, I guess I agree that this is all a little spooky," she said. "But I still don't think Dr. Cula is a vampire. I don't believe in vampires, like I don't believe in ghosts."

"I don't believe in ghosts, either," Dink said. "But I do believe what I see.

I think we should go talk to Officer Fallon."

"Okay, let's go see if *he* believes in vampires," Ruth Rose said.

"Wait a sec," Josh said. He had finished weaving a loop of garlic stalks. It was too small to slide over his head, so he plopped it on top of his hair, like a crown. "How do I look?" he asked.

"Like a smelly salad," commented Dink.

CHAPTER 6

Josh called Pal and clipped the leash to his collar. "Mom, I'm going into town with Dink and Ruth Rose!" he called toward the vegetable garden.

His mom's face popped up. "Okay, but please don't stay long," she said. "I need you to watch the twins while I dash to the market later."

"Are you wearing your garlic to see Officer Fallon?" Ruth Rose asked.

Josh grinned. "Oops, I forgot." He laid the garlic crown on the picnic table. He broke off one garlic bulb and stuck it in his shirt pocket.

"No vampire dude is getting me!" Josh said.

The kids cut through the elementary school grounds to reach Main Street. Then they took a right on Oak Street and passed People's Pond on their way to the police station.

Pal tugged Josh toward the pond. He took a few laps of pond water, scaring a frog. The frog plopped into the water and disappeared.

They found Officer Fallon washing his cruiser behind the police station. He had removed his shoes and socks and rolled up his pant legs.

"Hey, kids. Hey, Pal," the police chief said. He dropped a sponge into a bucket, walked over to a bench, and sat down. "Have you come to help me wash my car?"

The kids sat on the lawn near the bench. Pal crawled under the bench and sighed.

"Your cruiser doesn't look very dirty," Ruth Rose observed.

Officer Fallon grinned. "It doesn't really need washing," he admitted. "I just wanted to come out here and get my feet wet."

He wiggled his toes in the grass. "Say, what's that smell?" Officer Fallon looked under the bench. "Has Pal been rolling in something?"

"It's garlic," Josh said. He pulled the bulb out of his pocket.

Officer Fallon raised his eyebrows. "What're you trying to do, keep vampires away?" he joked.

Dink nudged Josh's leg with his foot. "Tell him, Josh."

Josh put the garlic bulb back in his pocket. "We saw this creepy-looking guy in town," he said, then began telling Officer Fallon the story.

As he listened to the three kids, Officer Fallon leaned forward with his elbows on his knees. "Let me get this straight," he said. "This man in black went into Ellie's, but didn't come out again. And then you saw a Band-Aid on Ellie's neck?"

"The same thing happened when he went into the Book Nook," Dink said. "The guy had vanished, and Mr. Paskey had a Band-Aid on *his* neck!"

"We found out he's staying at the Shangri-la," Josh went on. "And guess what? Mr. Linkletter had on a Band-Aid, too!"

"The guy we saw signed into the hotel as Dr. A. Cula," Ruth Rose added. "And that spells *Dracula!*"

Officer Fallon's eyebrows shot up.

"Well, I'll be darned!" he said.

"That's why we think he's a vampire!" Josh continued.

Officer Fallon let one of his hands fall on Pal's head. He rubbed the dog's ears while he thought.

"I think I saw the same fellow in town," Officer Fallon said after a minute. "He looked familiar, somehow."

"I thought so, too!" Ruth Rose cried. "I could swear I've seen his face before today."

Officer Fallon stood up. He emptied his bucket and began hosing off his car. "Tell you what," he said. "I'll try to find this Dr. Cula and have a talk with him. Will you kids be around?"

"I'll be at home," Ruth Rose said. "I promised to help my mom clean up the basement."

"I have to baby-sit the twins," Josh said. He poked Dink. "And Dink is going to help me."

"I am?" said Dink.

Officer Fallon shut off the hose. "Okay, I'll let you know what I find out about your vampire," he said, winking at the kids.

Dink and Josh walked Ruth Rose to

her house on Woody Street. Ruth Rose's cat, Tiger, was lying on her front porch. Pal tugged on his leash and whined.

"If you hear anything from Officer Fallon, let me know," Ruth Rose said, picking up her cat.

"You too," Josh said. He patted the garlic bulb in his pocket. "Sure you don't want to borrow this?"

"No thanks," Ruth Rose said. "Tiger here will protect me." She kissed her cat on the nose and opened her front door.

Dink, Josh, and Pal headed up Farm Lane. They were at Josh's house a few minutes later, and Josh let Pal off his leash.

The boys walked around to the back of the house and entered the kitchen.

"Hi, Mrs. Pinto," Dink said.

"Hello, Dink. Thanks for coming right back, Joshua," his mom said, grabbing her car keys. "The boys are waiting for

you in the barn. They want a ride on Polly."

"Cool," Josh said. He and Dink walked through the garden. Josh pulled up a carrot and wiped the dirt off on his shorts.

Inside the barn, Brian and Bradley were brushing Polly the pony.

"Yay! You're here!" Brian yelled. "I want to ride Polly first!"

"No, me first," cried Bradley. "I'm a minute older than you!"

Josh fed Polly the carrot and rubbed her velvety nose. "You can both ride at the same time," he said.

"But I get to ride in front!" Brian said.

"No, I'm oldest," said Bradley. "I get to ride in front."

Josh looked at Dink. "Help me," he begged.

CHAPTER 7

"How about if I flip a coin?" Dink asked. He pulled a quarter from his pocket. "Winner gets to choose who rides in front."

"I'll take heads," Brian said.

"So you can have tails," Dink told Bradley. He flipped the coin in the air and caught it. "It's tails."

"Good, I ride in front!" Bradley said. "I get to steer!"

"Riding in back is good, too," Dink said to Brian. "You get to enjoy the ride but don't have to do any work!"

"Thanks, Dink," Josh said. He led

Polly to an upside-down wooden box. Bradley climbed on the box, then Josh boosted him onto Polly's bare back.

Dink helped Brian up behind his twin brother. "Hold on to Bradley," Dink said.

"Let's run fast!" Bradley yelled.

"We're not running," Josh said. "We'll take a nice walk down to the river and back. Don't fall off, you monkeys!"

"We're not monkeys!" yelled Brian. "We're cowboys!"

Holding Polly's lead, Josh walked her into the meadow behind the barn. Dink walked next to the pony, making sure the boys didn't lose their seats.

Polly clopped along, dipping her head to munch the tops of weeds. Soon they crossed River Road and stopped on a grassy bank of the Indian River.

"Can we go swimming?" Bradley asked as Polly dipped her muzzle into the water.

"No, we're going back home as soon as Polly gets her drink," Josh said.

He and Dink sat on the grass and watched Polly drink.

"I wonder if Officer Fallon found out anything about Dr. Cula," Josh said, keeping his voice low so the twins wouldn't hear.

The boys sat and thought about the strange man in black.

"I've been thinking about those Band-Aids," Dink said.

"What about them?" Josh asked.

"They were all the same," Dink replied. "Why would three different people all have the exact same kind of round Band-Aid on their neck?"

"That *is* weird," Josh said after a minute. "You'd think one person might choose a round one but someone else would choose a regular strip, right?"

"Right," Dink said.

"We're thirsty!" Bradley yelled from Polly's back.

Josh stood up and gently pulled Polly's head away from the water. "Let's go home, girl," he said.

Soon they were back at the barn. Dink helped Brian and Bradley off Polly's back, and the twins raced toward the house.

"Let's go call Ruth Rose and see if she heard from Officer Fallon," Josh said as he let Polly into the corral.

Dink and Josh walked across the yard to the kitchen door. The twins were standing in front of the open refrigerator fighting over a carton of apple juice.

"Freeze!" Josh yelled.

The boys turned to look at him.

"Okay, now please hand me the juice, wash your hands, and sit," Josh said.

The twins did as they were told, and Josh poured four glasses of juice. He got a box of cookies from a shelf and gave each boy one.

Josh and Dink took their snacks over to the telephone on the hall table.

The light on the answering machine was blinking. "Maybe it's a message from Officer Fallon," Josh said.

He hit the PLAY button. But instead of the police chief's voice, they heard Ruth Rose. She said, "Guys, I figured it out! Meet me at the Shangri-la!"

Josh looked at Dink. "Figured out what?" he asked.

"Maybe she figured out who your mystery man is," Dink said. "Remember, she thought he looked familiar."

"So why did she go to the hotel without us?" Josh asked.

"She didn't know we'd be going to the river," Dink said.

"Well, let's go meet her," Josh said, heading for the kitchen. "Before the vampire gets her!"

Dink shook his head. "We can't leave your brothers alone," he said.

The twins had finished their juice and cookies. Josh looked out the window over the sink. "Come on, Mom," he said.

"Can we go out and play?" Bradley asked.

"After you put your glasses in the sink," Josh told the twins.

Just then Josh's mom pulled into the backyard and parked the car. Josh waved to her as Brian and Bradley shot out the back door.

"What did you bring us?" they yelled at their mother.

"Come on, out the front!" Josh whispered to Dink.

He and Dink left by the front door

and headed for Main Street. They cut through the high school grounds, then waved to Howard in his barbershop when they reached Main.

As they passed the Book Nook, Dink noticed that the shade was pulled down. A CLOSED sign was stuck in the window.

"Huh," Josh said, nodding toward the sign. "Mr. Paskey never closes in the middle of the afternoon."

Dink remembered that little, round Band-Aid on Mr. Paskey's neck. Then he shook his head. *No*, he thought. *There are no vampires in Green Lawn!*

CHAPTER 8

A few minutes later, Dink and Josh walked into the lobby of the Shangri-la Hotel. Mr. Linkletter was standing behind his counter, staring at the door.

"Hi, Mr. Linkletter," Josh said. "Ruth Rose said to meet her here. Have you seen her?"

Mr. Linkletter nodded. "Yes, I saw her about twenty minutes ago, with Dr. Cula."

Dink's eyes went to the little, round Band-Aid on Mr. Linkletter's neck. "Do you know where they went?" he asked.

"No, I didn't notice," Mr. Linkletter said. "They sat and talked here in the lobby. When I looked up again, they had disappeared."

Dink remembered how the mysterious man in black "disappeared" from Ellie's Diner and the Book Nook.

"Of course," Mr. Linkletter went on, "Dr. Cula could be up in his room. He likes to nap during the day."

Josh snuck a glance at Dink.

"Um, can you tell us which room he has?" Josh asked.

"That would be room 202," he said. "Feel free to go up and check."

Dink grabbed Josh by the arm and tugged him toward the elevators.

Dink pushed the UP button, and the boys waited. Seconds later, one of the two elevators arrived with a ping. Dink and Josh stepped inside.

"Did you see that?" Dink asked. "Mr.

Linkletter didn't even check his register. How did he know which room Dr. Cula had?"

"Yeah, and he never gives out room numbers," Josh said. "He always says guests at the Shangri-la pay for privacy."

"And did you notice how nervous he looked?" Dink said.

Josh nodded. "His mustache was practically doing a dance on his lip!"

The elevator pinged, and the doors slid open. Dink and Josh stepped into the long corridor and stood, listening. No one was in the hallway, and it was very quiet. The small wall lights cast a dim glow onto the carpet.

"This is creeping me out," Josh whispered. "What if that guy is in his room, just waiting for us?"

"Right now we have to find Ruth Rose," Dink said. He pointed to room 202. "Let's go."

They tiptoed toward the door. Dink

got ready to knock, then noticed that the door was already partly open.

He raised his eyebrows at Josh, who was staring back at him.

Dink pushed the door open a few more inches. "Dr. Cula?" he called through the crack. "Anyone here?"

No answer came. Josh nudged the door fully open with the toe of his sneaker.

There was no one in the room. The boys saw a TV set, a desk, an armchair, and night tables with lamps on both sides of a neatly made bed.

"It looks like no one is staying here," Dink said. "Mr. Linkletter did say room 202, right?"

Josh nodded. The boys tiptoed into the room for a better look.

Dink felt goose bumps marching up his arms and legs. Then he noticed a loud hum.

"The air conditioner is blasting," he

said to Josh with a shiver.

"It's freezing!" Josh answered. He walked across the room and stopped at the closet door. He looked at Dink. "Should I open it?"

Dink nodded.

Josh pulled the closet door open, then gasped.

"What?" Dink said, hurrying over for a look.

On the floor sat a black leather suitcase. Hanging above the suitcase on a hanger was a long black cape.

"He disappeared again," Josh whispered.

"Let's get out of here," Dink said. "We have to find Ruth Rose."

"Maybe she went back home," Josh suggested.

"Maybe," Dink said as they walked toward the door.

Against the wall to the right of the door was a small table they hadn't

noticed when they entered the room.

On it was a sheet of paper. A box of Band-Aids sat on top of the paper.

Dink picked up the Band-Aid box. "The little, round kind," he said, reading the words on the box.

"Oh my gosh!" Josh said, pointing to some writing on the paper.

Dink picked up the paper. "It's a list of names," he said.

He read the list out loud:

ELLIE LANDOLF ✓
ERNEST PASKEY ✓
LIONEL LINKLETTER ✓
RUTH ROSE HATHAWAY
DINK DUNCAN
JOSHUA PINTO

The names were written in purple. The first three names had purple check marks next to them.

"The vampire checked off the names of the people he bit on the neck!" Josh wailed. "And our names are next! I think I'm gonna be sick."

Dink studied the list. He was especially interested in the purple writing. Where had he seen that color before?

Then Dink remembered. He brought the paper up to his nose and took a deep sniff. He smiled.

"What do you smell?" Josh asked.

Dink grinned at his friend. "Jelly-beans," he said.

CHAPTER 9

"Jellybeans? What are you talking about?" Josh asked.

"I think Ruth Rose wrote this list," Dink said. "And she used Nate's Party Purple crayon."

"Oh, yeah, now I remember," Josh said. "But why would *she* make the list?"

"I don't know," Dink said. "And why did Mr. Linkletter let us come up here without giving us a hard time? Why was the door left partly open?"

"Unless Mr. Linkletter and this vampire guy are trying to pull something," Josh said.

Suddenly Josh grabbed Dink's arm. "Maybe Dr. Cula captured Ruth Rose and forced her to write this list!"

"I suppose that could have happened," Dink said. He picked up the Band-Aid box and emptied it onto the table. Each Band-Aid was wrapped in thin paper, but Dink could see the round shapes through the paper.

"You know what I think?" Dink asked.

Josh shook his head. "I can't think at all," he said. "My brain feels fried."

"I think these Band-Aids belong to Dr. Cula," Dink said. "And I think he gave one to Ellie. Then he gave Mr. Paskey and Mr. Linkletter theirs, too."

"After he bit their necks?" asked Josh.

"I don't think he bit anybody," Dink said.

"Then why would he give them Band-Aids?"

"Good question," Dink said. He set the box on top of the purple list. "And I think we'll get the answer when we find Ruth Rose."

Josh scratched his head. "But . . . that doesn't make any sense," he said. "How could Ruth Rose know anything? She's just as confused as we are about what's going on."

Dink shook his head. "No, her phone message said she'd figured it out," he said.

"So where is she?" Josh asked. "And where's the guy who checked into this room, whoever he is?"

"Well, they're not here," Dink said, glancing around the room. "Let's see if we can get any more information from Mr. Linkletter."

Just as the boys stepped through the door, they heard the ping of the elevator.

Dink yanked Josh back into the room. He shut the door, and they bolted toward the closet. The two boys jumped into the closet and pulled the door closed.

Inside the dark closet, Dink hid behind the cape, tugging Josh with him.

With their backs to the wall, they listened. Next to him, Dink felt Josh shaking.

Dink could hardly hear anything other than his own racing heartbeat. Then he heard a door open and close. Feet whispered across carpet. Something creaked, a chair or the bed. Then only silence.

"They're not here," Dink heard a voice whisper.

"Unless they're hiding in the closet," a different voice responded.

Dink tried to push through the wall behind him. He tried to shrink. He closed his eyes and willed himself to become invisible. Nothing worked.

Suddenly the door was yanked open.

"Come on out, you two," said a familiar voice.

Dink opened his eyes and peeked from behind the vampire's cape.

Ruth Rose was standing in the open closet doorway with a big grin on her face.

CHAPTER 10

Ruth Rose backed up as Dink and Josh stepped out of the closet. Behind her, five other people were in the room.

Ellie was leaning against the wall, wearing her uniform and apron.

Mr. Paskey and Mr. Linkletter were sitting on the edge of the bed.

Officer Fallon was sitting in the big chair in the corner.

The fifth person was Dr. A. Cula, dressed all in black. He had taken off his dark glasses and was sitting on the floor, leaning against the desk.

Everyone was smiling at Dink and

Josh and watching their faces.

"What's going on?" Josh asked.

The man in black stood up and stuck out his hand. "I'm Jimmy Jett," he said. "Hi, Dink. Hi, Josh."

Confused, Dink and Josh shook the man's hand.

"He's an actor, not a vampire," Ruth Rose said. She held up a magazine. It showed a picture of Jimmy Jett wearing the same black clothes. A caption read: JIMMY JETT JUMPS AT CHANCE TO PLAY DRACULA.

"I have a new movie coming out," Jimmy Jett said. "I play Dracula."

"Remember I said he looked familiar?" Ruth Rose asked. "I saw this when we were helping my mom with the old newspapers. I totally forgot until I saw Jimmy on TV when I went home after we talked to Officer Fallon."

Dink had a hundred questions, but he didn't know which one to ask first.

He did ask, "Can we sit down? I don't know about Josh, but my legs feel all wobbly."

Mr. Linkletter made room on the bed. "Sit here," he said.

After Dink and Josh were comfortable, Officer Fallon took over from Ruth Rose.

"When you kids left me, I came over here to meet this mysterious man in black." He waved at Jimmy Jett, who grinned. "I found him and Mr. Linkletter together, chatting like old friends. That's

when I learned that your 'vampire' was an actor from New York."

Jimmy made a little bow. "I'm sorry if I scared you kids," he said. "I was on my way to Vermont for a little vacation. Green Lawn looked like a nice place to stop, so I did. I went into the supermarket to buy a few things. When I saw you following me, I decided to have some fun."

"You knew we were following you?" Dink asked.

Jimmy grinned. "Oh, yes. I thought

you recognized me and that you knew about my new Dracula movie."

"But we didn't know," Josh said. "I thought you were a real vampire biting people's necks. We saw the Band-Aids!"

Jimmy nodded. "I always pack Band-Aids when I travel, in case I nick myself shaving," he said. "When I spotted you following me, I got an idea. That's why I went into Ellie's Diner."

Jimmy looked at Ellie. "You want to take over?" he asked.

Ellie smiled. "There I was, polishing my glass case," she said. "I looked up, and Jimmy Jett was standing in my diner! I recognized him right away and asked for his autograph."

"Instead, I handed her a Band-Aid," Jimmy said, cutting into Ellie's story. "I told her three kids were following me and I wanted to play a prank about being a vampire."

Ellie laughed. "I let Jimmy leave

through the back of the diner, and I stuck on the Band-Aid just as you kids walked in."

"The same thing happened to you, right, Mr. Paskey?" Dink asked.

Everyone looked at Mr. Paskey.

"That's right, Dink," he said. "Jimmy came in, explained who he was, and handed me a Band-Aid to put on my neck. He left through my back door just as you kids came in through the front."

Josh laughed. "Boy, were we fooled," he said to Jimmy.

"What about that book, *Vampires Among Us*?" Dink asked.

"I thought that would be a nice touch," Mr. Paskey said. "I lent the book to Jimmy, making it look as if he had taken it off my shelf and left the money for it."

"You guys are awesome!" Josh said.

Jimmy made a little bow. "The last step was when I got back to my hotel," he said. "Mr. Linkletter already knew who I was. I had signed in as Dr. A. Cula because I use that name in the movie."

Dink looked at Ruth Rose. "What about that list?" he asked. "And Nate's purple crayon?"

Ruth Rose laughed. "When I finally figured out who Dr. Cula really was, I came right here to the hotel," she said. "I had Nate's crayon in my pocket."

"And she forced me to tell all," the actor said with good humor. "I asked her if she'd like to help me with my prank."

"That's when I made that phone call to get you here," Ruth Rose said. "I wrote the list of names to scare you into thinking we were next!"

"And it worked!" Josh said.

"So you were all in it together," Dink said, looking at Officer Fallon. "Even you!"

"Only at the very end," Officer Fallon

said. "After Ruth Rose left her message on Josh's machine, I got Ellie and Mr. Paskey to join us here. Mr. Linkletter hid us all in his office until you'd gone up in the elevator."

A small smile appeared under Mr. Linkletter's mustache. "Will you boys forgive me?" he asked.

CHAPTER 11

The long black limo pulled up in front of a theater in New York City. The driver came around and opened the passenger door.

Dink, Josh, and Ruth Rose stepped out onto the sidewalk.

"Please wait here for your escort," the driver told the kids. "I'll be back after the movie to pick you up."

The kids thanked the driver and watched him pull the long limo back into traffic.

"This is so cool," Josh said. All around him people were streaming into

the theater. Over their heads a large marquee announced the name of the movie: **DRACULA'S DAUGHTER**.

"It was nice of Jimmy to invite us," Ruth Rose said.

"And feed us!" Josh said, patting his stomach. "I never had a picnic in a limo before."

"Maybe this is our escort," Dink said as a woman in a red uniform approached them.

"Are you Mr. Jett's friends from Connecticut?" she asked.

"Yes!" said Ruth Rose.

"Great, then follow me," the woman said. She led them into the theater and then to a bank of elevators.

"You'll be sitting in a special viewing box," the woman said as their elevator rose.

The elevator stopped, and the kids followed the escort down a quiet carpeted hallway to a small door. "Right in here," she said, and pushed the door open.

The kids walked into a small room with four seats. From here, the kids could see the screen and the rest of the audience.

"Enjoy the movie," the woman said. She closed the door and left them alone in the box seats.

The kids sat in the comfortable seats and looked around. On both sides, velvet drapes separated them from people in other box seats.

"I just can't believe we're actually

here," Josh whispered with awe.

"We wouldn't be if you hadn't seen Jimmy Jett in the supermarket," Ruth Rose said.

"Admit it," Dink said to Josh with a grin. "Did you really think he was a vampire?"

Before Josh could answer, the theater lights dimmed. Down below, the audience became quiet.

The curtain in front of the screen slowly parted, and creepy music began to play.

Behind the kids, the small door opened again. A man in a black cape entered the box. He sat down in the fourth seat, which happened to be next to Josh.

Josh turned. "Is that you, Jimmy?" he asked.

The man smiled, revealing long white fangs.

Dink gasped, and Ruth Rose giggled.

The man took out his fake fangs.
"Yeah, it's me," Jimmy Jett said. "I brought
these for you." He reached into a pocket
and pulled out three sets of vampire
fangs.

Dink, Josh, and Ruth Rose slipped
the fangs into their mouths just as the
movie started.

About the Author

Ron Roy is the author of more than fifty books for children, including the bestselling A to Z Mysteries® and the brand-new Capital Mysteries series. He lives in a very old farmhouse in Connecticut with his dog, Pal. When he's not writing about his favorite kids in Green Lawn, Connecticut, and Washington, D.C., Ron spends time restoring his house, gardening, and traveling all over the country.